MW01131621

EEK! Said Amy

Copyright © 2018 Abingdon Press
All rights reserved.

No part of this work may be reproduced or transmitted in any form or by any means, electronic or mechanical, including photocopying and recording, or by any information storage or retrieval system, except as may be expressly permitted by the 1976 Copyright Act or in writing from the publisher. Requests for permission can be addressed to Permissions, The United Methodist Publishing House, PO Box 280988, 2222 Rosa L. Parks Blvd., Nashville, TN 37228-0988 or e-mailed to permissions@umpublishing.org.

ISBN 978-1-5018-58659
PACP10528221-01

18 19 20 21 22 23 24 25 26 27— 10 9 8 7 6 5 4 3 2 1
MANUFACTURED IN THE UNITED STATES OF AMERICA

At the time of this book's publication, all facts and figures cited are the most current available. All telephone numbers, addresses, and website URLs are accurate and active; all publications, organizations, websites, and other resources exist as described in this book; and all have been verified as of December 2017. The author and The United Methodist Publishing House make no warranty or guarantee concerning the information and materials given out by organizations or content found at websites, and we are not responsible for any changes that occur after this book's publication. If you find an error or believe that a resource listed here is not as described, please contact The United Methodist Publishing House. Parents, teachers, and other adults: We strongly urge you to monitor children's use of the Internet.

Illustration by Charles Long. Watercolor backgrounds and additional cover graphics © Shutterstock, Inc.

EEK!
Said Amy

WRITTEN BY **L. J. Zimmerman**

ILLUSTRATED BY *Charles Long*

Abingdon Press · Nashville

Hi, I'm Devon.

This is my friend Amy.
She's an amygdala (pronounced uh-MIG-da-luh).

Amy lives in my brain.
She has a very
important job.
She helps me feel emotions.

6

Like happiness.

And sadness.

And anger.

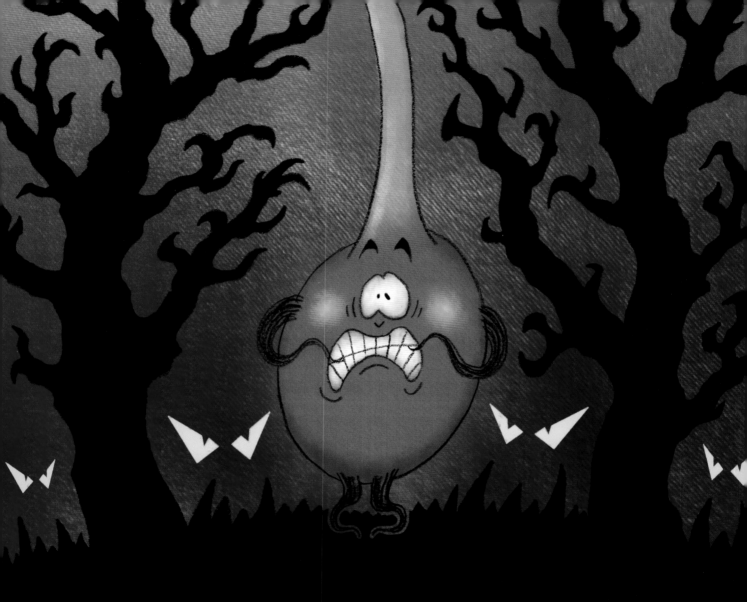

And fear.

Fear isn't fun.

But it's important.

13

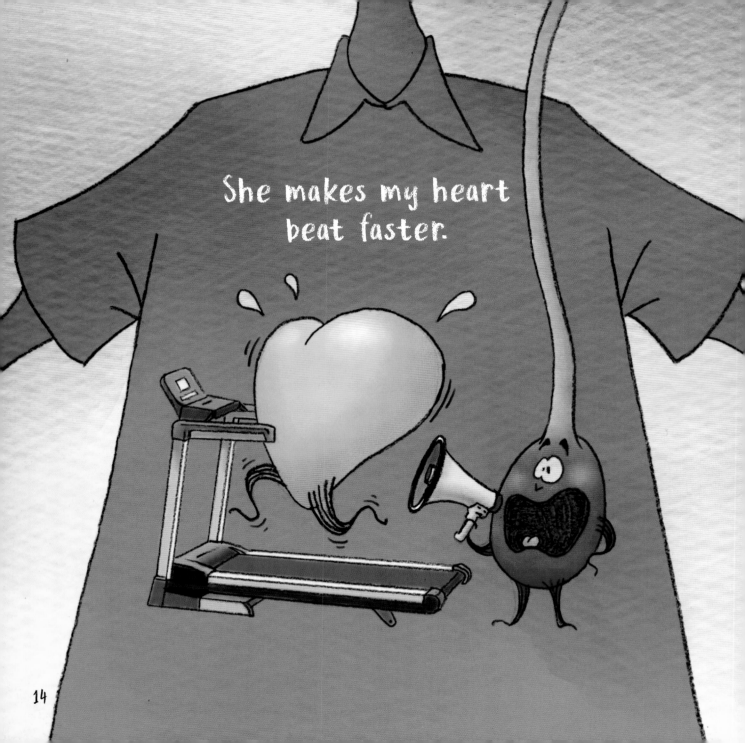

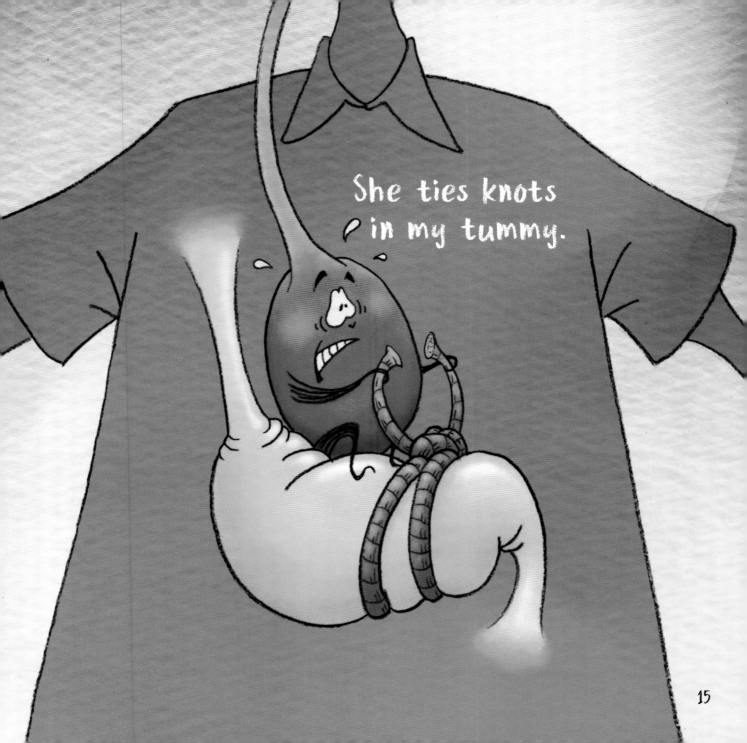

Or fight.

Amy and I make a great team.

Most of the time.

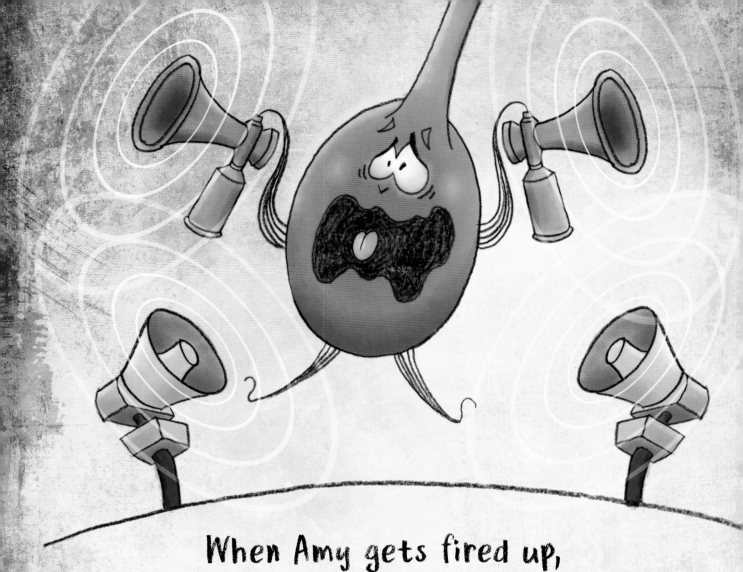

When Amy gets fired up,
it's hard to calm her down.

She's on red alert.

When Amy's on red alert, things that
are only a little scary

become SUPER scary.

When Amy's on red alert, I start to worry about stuff that I know doesn't make sense.

Mom helped me figure out how to calm Amy down when she's on red alert.

Now when Amy is on red alert,
I take a deep breath.
I imagine God's love filling me up.

Then I let it all out. I imagine all the scary feelings leaving my body.

I keep going until Amy calms down.

My dad helped me learn Bible
verses to say when
I'm scared.

Now when Amy's on red alert,
I say Psalm 23.

She seems to like it.

Sometimes it helps to thank Amy
for all her hard work.

God gave her a very important job,
after all.

But sometimes I have to be brave
to face my fears.

Amy understands.

I'm glad God gave me Amy
to show me how to be afraid.

And how to be brave.

Bible Verses to Say When You Are Scared

Exodus 14:13–14

Psalm 23

Psalm 46:1–2

Isaiah 41:10

Mark 5:36

John 14:25–27

Romans 8:38–39

2 Timothy 1:7

Hebrews 13:6

In this day and age, raising children to be courageous and compassionate feels harder than ever. News of conflict, war, and violence in society seems to bombard us from all sides, and makes the task of keeping our children safe, both mentally and physically, feel nearly impossible.

While we can't entirely protect our children from seeing or hearing scary things—on the news, on the bus ride home, or at a friend's house—we can help our children process and cope with what scares them. For young children, it can be helpful to talk with them about scary images or stories they hear and help them identify whether those fears are based in reality.

Unfortunately, some fears are based in reality. Many children cope with these fears in healthy ways. Sometimes, a child's form of coping can become unhealthy. Fears can develop into phobias, taking up a disproportionate amount of the child's emotional energy. Fears can cause obsessive thoughts and compulsive reactions, such as checking and re-checking locks, lights, or homework. Fears can cause a constant, low-level anxiety that something bad will happen.

There are many healthy ways of expressing and facing fears, some of which are named in this book. You can help your child name his or her fears and develop strategies for dealing with them. Below are a few resources to help you learn more about healthy ways to respond to fear and anxiety. If your child's way of coping with fear begins to disrupt her or his daily life, it's important to seek professional help.

- National Association for the Education of Young Children, "Coping with Violence," *https://www.naeyc.org/our-work/families/coping-with-violence*

- Dawn Huebner, PhD, *What to Do When You Worry Too Much: A Kid's Guide to Overcoming Anxiety* (Washington, DC: Magination Press, 2005).

- James J. Crist, PhD, *What to Do When You're Scared and Worried: A Guide for Kids* (Minneapolis, MN: Free Spirit Publishing, 2014).